Naughty Dogs

© 2023 Peter S. Fischer
Herstellung und Verlag: BoD – Books on
Demand, Norderstedt
ISBN: 9783751932684

The Book

Every dog owner is convinced of their furry friend's good behavior and will claim: "My dog is well-behaved and properly trained!" But is he really? When walking him? When visiting a friend's apartment with him? When entering a business with him? When going to a restaurant and bringing him along? When driving in the car with him? When, for example, you tie him up outside a bakery?

These are just a few examples that can lead to great entertainment and, afterwards, worries if your beloved pet doesn't do what is expected of him. I'm sure it never gets boring. He looks at you sweetly and claims, "I didn't do anything, I was good the whole time. Can I have my treat now?" And you're boiling with anger. Whether big or small, it doesn't matter; in some matters, they're all the same. If you don't pay attention in time, they can be like small children and do whatever they want. If they're not properly trained?

I spent a lot of time with a German Shepherd during my childhood, so it was clear that when I grew up, I had to have a dog and would always have an additional family member. With them, I experienced many funny or not-so-nice moments.

While walking the dog, you always meet some dog owners who tell you about their pets' experiences. I usually don't know these people's names, but I know the name of their dog. It's true, when my wife and I are out for a walk, we might say, "There's Maxi and his owner." But you don't always have to know everyone so well. The dogs know each other well, they know the different owners, and they know how to outsmart them.

Peter S. Fischer

Naughty Dogs

25 Funny Stories About Dogs

Volume 1

Edited by Elfriede Denk

If a dog could write books, what would he write about his owner?

Peter S. Fischer

1. Story

My First Dog

My first dog was a female Yorkshire Terrier named Aischa. She was from a breeder and was a bit too big for the typical Yorkshire Terrier, so no one wanted her. That's why she immediately caught my eye and found a proper home with me. She was such a sweetheart.

One time, I had a funny experience with her. We were having a big family celebration in our garden. We were all having a great time grilling, and I had a little keg of beer for the guests. Unfortunately, the tap was leaking, so we decided to just put a bowl under it. We continued to grill, and my lovely dog got some scraps from the table. I've never been too strict about what my dog eats, as long as she doesn't beg or jump on the table. It's not fair to watch all that delicious food and not be able to have any. Imagine being hungry and standing in front of a grill, unable to eat anything. Of course, my dog didn't get any seasoned meat; she had her own unseasoned meat.

But after a while, I noticed that my dog had disappeared. I couldn't see or hear her anywhere. That was strange. I searched the garden and all the rooms in the house, and then I found her sleeping on the couch in the children's room. This was unusual behavior for her. I was wondering how she could fall asleep like this, as she never did before. Then my wife told me that the bowl of beer from the keg was empty. We all realized why our dog was sleeping so soundly. Normally, she would stay with the guests until the end of the party, making sure not to miss anything. She was more than just curious. So we had to continue the party without our dog, who was now drunk and couldn't be awakened.

The next morning, my dog and I always went for a walk at the same time. However, she was still sleeping, and I thought it would be better if we went outside. She looked at me briefly and then put her head back down. It was like she was saying, "You can go outside and pee by yourself today. I'm sick." I gently picked her up and put her on her wobbly legs. I could tell that my dog was really sick today. She didn't want to move much, and she probably had a severe headache. It was clear that my dog had a real hangover. She moved slowly and carefully outside, and I realized that this walk would take longer than usual.

Personally, I wasn't feeling great either. When my wife got up, she immediately tended to the poor, sick dog. Aischa was heavily pitied and petted.

But what about me? I also had some pain from the party, but I was simply told it was my own fault. Sometimes, it seems like dogs have it easier with women. But from then on, we made sure Aischa didn't get any more beer. We couldn't let something like that happen again!

The dog probably thought, "Whatever causes such bad headaches must be good, so I can't be naughty!"

2. Story

The Trip

It was a beautiful weekend, my wife wanted us to take a trip to Bad Wörishofen on Sunday, which was not a long drive away. So, my wife said that our furry companion should be bathed and brushed on Saturday evening. She showered our little four-legged friend with a special shampoo for dogs, which the Dame absolutely did not like, and she wanted to jump out of the bathtub right away. But she loved the blow-drying so much that my wife always dried her a bit longer. She would lift her head in a way that she wanted the warm stream of air from the dryer. Her face would beam with joy during the process. The next day, after lunch, we drove to the Kneipp town and had a nice day with a long hike followed by coffee. Our dog walked very obediently the whole way.

As we left the café, we decided to walk to the car and take a little detour. We passed by a field where a farmer had apparently just spread fresh manure. We didn't have our dog on a leash. What we saw was unbelievable. Our freshly bathed dog ran into the foul-smelling field and rolled around in the fresh dung, writhing with delight in the stinking muck. She didn't want to stop rolling around in the dirt. She looked very happy, but we did not. Yelling and scolding didn't help at all, and running into the field wouldn't have been sensible in this case. When our dog thought she was done, she ran back to us, overjoyed. She stood in front of us, grinning, and asked for praise. But the dog certainly didn't receive any praise. My wife scolded her, the dog smelled terrible, and we had to drive home with her. But we were lucky that we passed by a lake, and fortunately there were no bathers present, so I chased the dog into the lake. But we had to discover in the car that our dog still smelled terrible. We drove home with the windows open, which didn't seem to bother our dog at all. She acted as if nothing had happened, thinking it was still a beautiful outing. Every perfume would have been useless. Our dog had thoroughly enjoyed it. When we arrived home, my wife immediately grabbed our dog and scrubbed all the stinky dirt out of her dense fur, but this time, my wife did it very carefully and for a little longer. And she dried her hair for a shorter period. You could say it was still a beautiful dog outing, and everyone got what they wanted.

She kept trying, the beautiful scent seemed to attract her irresistibly. At first, it was a game to see who smelled it first, her or her owner. But later on, she learned that we didn't want her to roll in the dirt, or was it the dreaded bath?

We realized we weren't alone in this problem. Other dog owners we knew had gone through something similar. It seems that the dirt and smell are like perfume to dogs. They want their whole body to smell like it. Well, I can think of much better scents.

The dog must be thinking, "You don't know what smells good, do you? How can I be a bad dog if I enjoy this?"

3. Story

Vacation by the Sea

Let me tell you about our Yorkshire Terrier. My wife and I decided to take a vacation with our car and bring our furry friend along. We chose to drive to Pesaro on the Adriatic coast at the end of September when it wouldn't be too hot for our Aischa.

And so we did. The car ride and many kilometers didn't bother our Yorkshire Terrier at all. In fact, she loves riding in the car and was interested in everything she saw. She often didn't know where to look first. When it became too much for her, she lay down on the back shelf, where she had a good view. We stopped often so that everyone, especially our dog, could stretch their legs and take a break.

We finally arrived in Pesaro and settled into a dog-friendly hotel near the beach. Aischa was very excited when she saw the sea for the first time. She ran straight into the water, jumping around and snapping at the waves. It was wonderful to see how much joy she had.

Upon arriving in Pesaro, our Aischa was immediately greeted by our hotel owners' dog. The two dogs saw each other every day and got along well. We noticed that our dog was also on vacation here, as she had a lot to see and many different smells to take in. We walked around the whole town, and our Aischa didn't get tired at all. She systematically sniffed every corner and every tree. Whenever other dogs came around, she got very excited and had to meet them. Apparently, dogs and animals don't experience language barriers.

Early in the morning and late in the evening, we went for walks on the beach. This was new for Aischa, and she immediately wanted to run into the sea since she's a water rat. However, she didn't understand the waves and kept going back when one approached. She looked at me, as if to say, "What's this? The water is moving. That's impossible." But after a while, she overcame her hesitation and walked cautiously into the water and had fun. Then I had to keep throwing her ball, and she didn't want to get out of the water. She kept bringing the ball back and wanting me to throw it again and again.

One late evening while we were taking a walk on the beach, Aischa naturally wanted to go into the sea again and I had to throw her ball. All the boats had already been tied up, and some had small balls attached to their ropes. Our dog saw these balls and immediately wanted one, but this ball just wouldn't come with her. After a few minutes, she became angry, growling and barking at the little ball on the rope, biting it over and over again, but she just couldn't take it with her. Then she looked at the ball in surprise, not understanding the world anymore. We called to her again and again, but she refused to come out of the water without that ball. Another dog owner, an Italian from the town, watched the spectacle with us. We had to laugh, but we also saw that the little one couldn't be gotten out of the water anymore.

He threw his dog's ball right next to ours, which Aischa immediately grabbed, and she came out of the water completely exhausted. Now she had her ball, and she wouldn't let anyone take it from her.

The Italian said he had plenty of tennis balls as he worked at a tennis court. We met almost every day of the vacation on the beach, and of course, Aischa had to be there, and everyone had fun!

But was Aischa a naughty dog? My dog claimed that the ball was naughty; it was her ball that she found!

4. Story
Duck Hunting

Every day, we took our Yorkshire Terrier for a walk, even on a very cold winter day. We chose a beautiful lake to go for a walk as usual. We had a ball with us, so that our Aischa wouldn't get bored. She kept fetching the ball and never seemed to get enough of it. When ducks were sitting on the shore, she ran to the lake and chased them into the water with wild barking. You could have thought that the cunning ducks were quacking, "follow us into the water, you won't catch us anyway." So we played ball a few more times.

The ducks had reassembled on the shore, and my silly dog fell for their trick and actually chased the ducks into the icy water. We shouted after Aischa, but her hunting instinct was much stronger. The dog's mind must have been completely switched off in that moment. She couldn't hear anything and apparently only saw the ducks. She swam a few meters after the birds, who were having a good laugh at our little dog and literally mocking her with loud cackles. My little dog must have realized how terribly cold the water was. She paddled back a few meters and just stood in the shallow, icy water, not going any further. We called out to her, but she didn't take another step. I had no choice but to take off my shoes and socks, roll up my pants, and step into the shallow, icy water to rescue our dog. The dog was shaking all over, and her entire fur had become completely stiff.

The owner was now also shaking all over, my feet were freezing. I handed the stiff dog to my wife, quickly put on my socks and shoes, and we ran with our little polar bear to the car, wrapped her in a blanket, and quickly started the car. The heater was turned up to full heat. I could barely feel my feet for a few minutes. It was an involuntary Kneipp cure and much too cold. I think the ducks must have been laughing their heads off at me and my dog, and they still tell the story to this day.

At home, our dog, which was not always the case, was given a warm shower, brushed and pleasantly blow-dried, which was very nice for the pretty Yorkshire lady in this case. For the dog, the world was back in order. Since that day, I didn't have to teach Aischa to stop chasing ducks anymore. She marched past them, ignoring them, not giving them a second glance. She wanted to show them that she was over it and that they couldn't lure her into the icy water anymore.

Was this a lesson for the dog, like for little children? Apparently, it had worked! This experience remained in our memory for a long time.

In that moment, the dog must have thought, "I'm not going to let myself be laughed at by such stupid birds. I'll show them what a real dog is. That doesn't make me an unruly dog, does it!"

5. Story
Grilling by the Riverbank

A friend told us about how she went for a walk with her young Golden Retriever on a hot summer evening by the river, and the dog had a blast splashing around in the cool water, not wanting to leave.

She met many other dog owners, chatted and exchanged experiences, and everything was very relaxed. But suddenly, the young Golden Retriever lifted his nose in the air, having caught a scent of something. Someone was grilling nearby.

If the dog could draw, he could sketch every grill by the river and what delicious treats were on them. In his mind, a clear menu of grilled foods was passing by, with many tasty sausages and meats.

The nose briefly went in one direction and shortly after, the whole body followed. Our friend immediately interrupted the conversation and shouted after her dog, but the dog only knew one direction - the very enticing smell of a grill. The good sausages and fine grilled meat were certainly more appealing than the usual dog food. No matter how much the friend shouted, the dog paid no attention to her anymore. Suddenly, the dog disappeared towards a large gravel bank where a wood-fired grill and some men were standing. As they saw the dog rushing towards them, they knew immediately what he wanted - he was hungry, very hungry, with drool already running out of his mouth. Despite the men trying to chase him away, the dog managed to steal some meat from the wood-fired grill without burning his mouth. With a few greedy bites, the grilled food disappeared into his large mouth. The friend arrived at the gravel bank exhausted, but the dog was waiting for her with great joy and said, "There is good food, I saved some for you." However, the men had a different opinion. Luckily, the friend knew all the men slightly, and they suggested she quickly go shopping and bring back at least a case of beer as compensation.

Since she was so out of breath, she explained to her husband over the phone what had happened and asked him to quickly get something and bring it to the men. She naturally brought the misbehaving dog back home.

Her husband quickly went shopping. He brought fresh grilled food and a crate of beer with him to the gravel bank with their dog. What happened next? The dog disappeared, and so did the man.

The next day, his wife asked him what had happened and why he hadn't come back sooner. Her husband replied, "It was the dog's fault, he didn't want to leave the grill." The dog is always misbehaving! The woman then asked, "Did our dog also drink a few bottles of beer?"

The dog thought to himself, if they grill more often, then I won't be an unruly dog, my master enjoyed it too!

6. Story

The Restaurant

I cannot withhold this short story from you that a friend of mine from our dog scene told me while we were walking our dogs. This man used to go alone with his dog to a restaurant, which he visited regularly. He apparently owned a very large dog, from the description I would say it was probably a Doberman. The dog sat very obediently next to his owner, who read his menu and then ordered his beer and food. In the meantime, the dog lay very bored on the ground. The owner waited for his food and drank his beer on the side, but the food did not come as quickly today, so he ordered his second beer in the meantime. The dog was still lying very bored on the ground. But the owner had almost finished his second beer and the food still hadn't arrived.

However, the owner had drunk a lot of beer by now and therefore had a strong urge to pee. He told his dog, who was still very bored on the ground: "He should be good!" The owner quickly went to the bathroom and emptied his bladder, hoping that his food would finally arrive. He had ordered a nice pork roast with dumplings.

In the meantime, the waiter brought the desired food and placed it on the table next to the partially drunk beer. The dog was no longer lying so bored. His keen sense of smell went up and he wondered what his owner had ordered today.

When the waiter left the table, the dog's previously bored body rose up and he looked more closely at his owner's food. The owner wondered if he really wanted the strange food, thinking that it would probably be cold by the time it arrived. The big mouth of the dog briefly opened and suddenly the pork roast disappeared, but the nice big dumpling was still on the plate. The dog now lay down again, looking bored. The owner arrived and immediately ordered another beer on the way. When he sat down to his pork roast, he probably thought that he had not ordered anything vegetarian. But by now, the waiter had arrived with the third beer and said, "You ate quickly today, don't you like the dumpling?"

The dog sat up and looked at the waiter, saying, "It was good, but it could be a bit more. But my owner pays!" The dog thought, "I wasn't at fault, my owner left, who else was going to eat all this? I just helped out. So I'm not an ill-behaved dog!"

7. Story

Dachshund Mixes

After my Yorkshire Terrier, I brought two Dachshund mixes into the house from a litter. It was a poor sibling pair rescued from a laboratory by a woman. It was a male and a female. We only wanted one dog, but the woman didn't want them to be separated.

Now, there was real life in the apartment, and I quickly realized that it was very difficult to train them. We named them Trixi and Rocky. If one dog focused on me, the other would act silly and want to play. So, I started doing individual training later on. I immediately realized that I was reaching my limits in training them. They formed their own pack and always wanted to do what they wanted to do. Just as I taught one dog something, the other one would do the opposite. Sometimes I was very close to losing my patience. While Dachshunds were stubborn by nature, it was even more difficult with two of them. But with time and a lot of patience, we managed to get the two little devils to obey a bit, to come back to us when we let them run free and called them. But this training was the most intensive; it required a lot of patience and nerves of steel. One of them always ignored my call. Usually, one would listen and come in my direction, and the other would say, "I don't feel like it today," suddenly turning back and starting to wrestle with the other. But as I said, we eventually managed to train them.

We went on a beautiful forest walk and searched for mushrooms along the way. The two dogs were running wild through the woods, but always stayed within sight. I called them back to us from time to time and they obediently sat in front of us. We were very proud that they were following our commands. However, we didn't think about the fact that the two Dachshund mixes were also hunting dogs and there was other wildlife in the forest. Suddenly, a rabbit darted out and ran away quickly. Our dogs thought, if the rabbit can run so fast, we should chase after it too. Suddenly, we were alone and the dogs were nowhere to be seen, only the sound of their barking could be heard. We called out to them and tried to lure them back to us. After a while, Rocky slowly returned and sat obediently in front of us. We praised him for coming back so quickly, but Trixi was still nowhere to be seen and we didn't hear anything from her. We desperately continued to call out for her and searched through the forest for over an hour.

After a long search, we saw the naughty lady sitting on a dirt road, just looking at us. We immediately examined the young lady and found that Trixi's nose was a little swollen, she was most likely stung by a wasp and had a sting on her hindquarters. Not far from Trixi, we discovered a ground wasp nest. Had the little one stuck her nose in there? Then it's no wonder her nose was swollen and she got stung on her butt. The wasps had defended their nest. Trixi probably won't stick her nose curiously everywhere anymore.

That wouldn't be such a bad thing for some people to do too.

Trixi probably thought, if the wasps fly in there, there must be a reason for it, so let me take a closer look. Am I naughty because of that?

8. Story
Grandma and Grandpa

 I remember everything very clearly. My grandparents had a very large German Shepherd. I was still very young and not yet in school. The big German Shepherd, named Rolf, was my best friend and I could do everything with him, except take away his bones, which he immediately corrected me for, he didn't like that!

 When I stayed overnight with my grandfather, Rolf slept right next to my bed until I fell asleep. Then he sneaked away to his place. He had his place and a big dog bed in the hallway. Rolf had it good in a 1200 square meter garden, with plenty of space to run around. But sometimes he was also a rascal. On weekends, my grandma often prepared my favorite dish, apple fritters, crispy baked in a Jena glass. But it was also Rolf's favorite dish, and usually my parents, aunt, and uncle were present for this meal. Rolf couldn't be pulled away from the kitchen when grandma was cooking. He nervously followed everything grandma was doing, and couldn't wait for the apple fritters to come to the table. Rolf whined until he got something in his bowl. After a few seconds, Rolf had devoured it and was immediately back at the table whining again. He thought the little bite he had gotten was for his bad tooth. Grandma pushed him aside and said, "He's already had something and that has to be enough." Rolf wasn't quite satisfied yet and sneaked over to my uncle and sat down right next to him. He watched my uncle eat closely, every movement following his eyes, his head always moving with him. But my uncle didn't react to Rolf. After a few minutes, Rolf started to whine and made himself noticed, pushing him continuously with his head.

My uncle still didn't react. Then Rolf lowered his head, under the arm where my uncle held his fork. Rolf skillfully waited until my uncle had speared a large piece with the fork. Rolf didn't take his eyes off the delicious apple fritter for a second. My uncle brought the fork to his mouth. Now was Rolf's moment, his skull shot up quickly and with the jolt, my uncle lost his good piece of apple fritter from the fork and it fell onto his pants and onto the floor. Rolf's trick had worked and he eagerly grabbed the good piece.

Grandma scolded him immediately and he had to go out into the hallway. But two minutes later he sneaked back in and sat down next to my uncle again, maybe the trick will work again, bad dog? Rolf could be scolded as much as you wanted, but when there were apple fritters, he was crazy, otherwise he was meek.

Rolf said, "It fell on the floor, and what's on the floor is mine! Besides, it's my favorite food. I'll leave you some because I'm so kind!"

Is he a naughty dog?

9. Story

The dog, my friend and protector

Many dogs need a purpose, which is why it often happens that if they don't have one, they seek and take on one themselves. Most of the time, it's to protect their owner and their territory.

So, I heard a story from a former colleague. He was out for a few beers with some colleagues. His wife and their big dog stayed at home. Late at night, the man came home slightly drunk. He undressed and was surprised that his dog didn't greet him. He didn't turn on the light so as not to wake his wife, and when he pulled back the covers on the bed, he suddenly heard a menacing growl. He immediately tried to chase his dog out of the bed, but to no avail. The dog started to bark and growl even more. His wife woke up and said, "I think you'll have to sleep off your drunk on the couch tonight. First come, first served." Who is the villain in this case? The man who came home drunk or the dog who had taken his place, his wife who let the dog in the bed and didn't correct him?

The dog then grew into his role. Nobody was allowed to get too close to his wife. Even people who just wanted to shake her hand or make a gesture in her direction were immediately growled at by the big dog. Even his owner had problems with his dog. The dog no longer knew where his limits were and didn't allow anyone near his mistress anymore.
So it happened as it had to happen, when a woman wanted to shake hands with the owner, the dog immediately bit her. Later, he also tried to bite his owners. For the dog, it is not a mistake, he thinks: "I just want to watch over my mistress and make sure nothing happens to her or comes too close to her." They waited too long to show the dog where his limits were. I don't know what happened to this dog, but it could easily be that this poor animal, who never received proper training, had to be put down.

It could also be that this owner is still sleeping on the couch and the big dog is sleeping next to his mistress, good night!

The dog thought only: "I just want to watch over my mistress, am I an ill-behaved dog because of that?"

10. Story

The Sleeping Man

I know another story that I experienced myself. It involves a man and his dog, a large Doberman that protected and guarded his owner. This experience was likely quite costly for the man. It's been many years since then, but an experience like that is not easily forgotten.

I was working the night shift at a tram workshop during a big festival. The trams were being brought into the storage hall when someone noticed that a very drunk man was sleeping in one of the cars, with his Doberman lying beside him. The driver who brought the tram in asked us if we could help wake the man up, but the man was completely unresponsive.

Our whole group followed the driver to the tram where we found the disheveled man asleep on the floor, with his dog right beside him. We tried nudging him to wake him up, but as we got closer, the dog began to growl and wouldn't let us near his owner. The size of the dog and his threatening behavior gave us great respect and made us realize that it would be best to keep our distance and find another solution.

We had no choice but to call the police, who arrived promptly. But even the police officers were unable to get close to the man. The dog showed no respect towards them and even threatened to bite them. The dog was fiercely guarding his owner, and no one was going to disturb his sleep.

So they had no choice but to call their dog unit, it didn't take long and they were quickly on the scene. Armed with treats and everything possible, they tried to outsmart the big and dangerous culprit. Meanwhile, the owner had been sleeping for a very long time and the dog made no attempt to let his owner move even one meter alone. The dog unit tried every trick possible, but no chance, the dog didn't move.

Until one of the police officers in the dog unit had an idea, that a colleague owned a female dog in heat, which they quickly brought. This pretty lady dog hadn't even jumped out of the car, and the Doberman's nose immediately went up and he came towards the fine lady dog. And the police were able to do their job and remove the heavily intoxicated man from the tram, most likely taking the man to a sobering-up cell. The dog followed his lady dog into the car.

What defines a woman, this dog had abandoned his owner completely for a four-legged lady. What had become of the dog and his owner, I could no longer find out, but one can imagine.

It probably would have been better if the dog had been the one drinking and the owner had been taking care of his dog.

Is this dog misbehaving because he followed an attractive lady dog and left his owner alone in his drunkenness?

The dog probably thought, "While my owner sleeps off his drunkenness, why not follow the beautiful lady and have some fun myself!"

11. Story

The Car Enthusiast

This is a story that was told to me and stuck in my memory because it was so extraordinary, but for the man who told it to me, it was very embarrassing at the time it happened. The longtime colleague had a very young German Shepherd at the time, and every weekend he would go to a dog school with him and, as he told me, had a very solid training. As always, he went out with his dog for the second time very long after breakfast so that the dog could really run around. He lived a little outside the city, so he let the dog chase through fields and meadows and really tire him out. He also threw him a stick. The fields and meadows were still very wet at this time, so his fur was quite dirty. He didn't really care about that in this moment, because his dog definitely needed a shower. So he slowly walked back with his exhausted, dirty German Shepherd.

When he returned to his house, his neighbor was standing behind his car with a brand-new Mercedes and wanted to show off his new acquisition. He immediately opened the car door to show him the inside of the noble car that my storyteller liked very much. They talked about the new car for a while and the car doors remained open. His dirty dog was still sitting next to him at that moment. In this moment, the well-trained dog thought to himself: "If that's the case and the doors are open, I'll jump right onto the back seat, because they're sure to take a test drive and I'll definitely be allowed to come along." When the trunk was opened, the men were stunned to see the dog sitting on the almost white leather backseat with its dirty fur and still feeling quite comfortable. My colleague had forgotten that his dog had a thing for cars, he loved to ride in them and my colleague had to be careful when a car door was open. His dog wanted to jump into this vehicle immediately and then wait for it to drive away. So also in this moment. He quickly pulled his dirty dog out of the brand-new car and they looked at the damage.

The car owner then had an interior cleaning done and the damage was fixed, the dog owner had of course received the bill and paid it, luckily he had a dog liability insurance and they had covered the bill. The test drive for the dog didn't happen!

The dog thought to himself, "If you like to ride in cars so much and obediently jump onto the back seat, then you're not an ill-behaved dog, right?" Next time, I'll just sit in the driver's seat right away!

12. Story

The Rabbit

This is a story from my surroundings and it is one of my personal favorite stories. A woman with a larger garden and a dog, which I assume was a breed with a strong hunting instinct. Unfortunately, I never found out what breed the dog was. In addition, the young woman had two smaller children. The neighbor bred rabbits and had very well-maintained stables and was very proud of his breeding. As I also learned, he went to exhibitions with these rabbits and had won several prizes.

The children were playing in the garden that day and, of course, the dog was with them. Suddenly, the children found one of these rabbits from the neighbor, completely dirty and no longer alive. It was a snow-white animal and apparently one of the

special rabbits that their neighbor had bred. The
mother of the children looked at the dead animal
with great shock and immediately suspected her dog
of having chased and killed a rabbit from the
neighbor.

 She sneaked into the neighbor's garden, the man
was not at home at this time, and inspected every
single stall. Indeed, one was empty. She came to the
conclusion that her dog had killed the rabbit. She
couldn't ask her husband what to do either, as he was
at work.

 So the mother and her children came to the
decision: "The rabbit must be washed and then
blow-dried, so that the special animal is clean
again." After that, the three sneaked into the rabbit
hutches and carefully placed the rabbit in the empty
hutch, as if it were sleeping. That same evening,
they saw a very upset neighbor. The woman asked
the man what was wrong, and he replied,
"Yesterday, I buried my very old rabbit that died a
natural death, and now the animal is clean, smelling
good, and blow-dried in its hutch. How can that be?
Something fishy is going on." The woman then told
him that she had found the rabbit totally dirty in her
garden and suspected her dog of killing it. Even the
rabbit breeder had to laugh and buried his dead

rabbit a second time, but in a secure place where the dog couldn't dig it up again.

The dog sat there completely indifferent and thought, "I just wanted to play with the rabbit. That doesn't make me an ill-behaved dog!"

13. Story

The Hospitable Dog

I had a very nice colleague who owned a house with a large garden, and of course, a bigger dog came with it, whom I already knew well from his stories. My colleague invited me over to his house after work, he was really keen on me getting to know his house and his dog. The dog greeted us at the garden gate, jumping up and down with excitement. His wife and the dog welcomed us with joy. I couldn't tell the breed of the dog, only that he was slightly smaller than a German Shepherd and a mix of many breeds. Nonetheless, he was a very sweet dog and looked quite funny as a mixed breed. He didn't leave our side for a minute and always wanted to be petted. Even during our snack, he got some good pieces, the dog was well taken care of.

 Then the moment came when I had to say goodbye, as I wanted to go home to my loved ones. My own dog was waiting for me and also wanted some attention. My colleague said, "I don't need to accompany you, you know where to go." The dog followed me to the garden gate, but just before, he stood in front of me, growled, and barked at me. He didn't want to let me leave. I tried to persuade him with kind words and petting, but the dog remained stubborn, and I was not allowed to leave the property. His wife and my colleague stood at the front door, watching the scene. They laughed at me and shouted, "Now you have to stay here and spend the night with us." He immediately came to me and took the dog with him, but the dog still followed his command and explained, "No one can easily slip out of the house. He lets everyone in, even strangers, but once they're on the property, they don't leave unless I want them to. I call him back or accompany the visitor to the garden gate!"

 He then said, "Burglars can easily enter his house, but they can't leave!" The dog thought, "Am I a naughty dog if I don't let anyone leave? I just want to be hospitable!"

14. Story

Excluded

A good acquaintance in our area owned a German Shepherd, and as befits such a large animal, had a house with a large garden. She regularly took the dog to a dog school. The dog was very well-behaved and obedient. He was allowed to roam freely in the house and garden.

The dog learned quickly and knew how to open doors if one was locked during his daily rounds. He stood briefly on his hind legs to push down the latch with his front paw and then pushed the door open with his snout. But what had gotten into the dog on this particular day is still unknown to the single woman. She only wanted to take out the trash and left the door open, and the German Shepherd followed her into the garden. A very good acquaintance passed by at that time, with whom she chatted briefly. When she turned around, she saw with great horror that her front door had slammed shut. But what calmed her down was that the dog was inside and she thought he knew how to open the door. The two women went to the front door and she called her dog to come outside and open the door. But the dog made no attempt to move. She looked through a window and saw the dog lying very relaxed in his dog bed, taking a nap. "He always ran outside immediately before to see what was going on," the woman said. The woman tried repeatedly to call her dog, but he simply wouldn't budge. For over an hour, the woman tried to get her dog to come outside.

It wasn't until a familiar man with his female dog in heat passed by that the dog suddenly jumped up, and there was a brief noise as the front door opened and the dog ran to greet his friend, wagging his tail. The woman went into her house with a shaking head and scolded, "I can call him all I want, but when a female dog in heat comes by, then he suddenly moves. That's going to be an extra hour in dog school." The man with his dog must still be laughing about the story today. The woman had the front door quickly modified, just in case it ever slammed shut again.

The dog said, "I learned that I should not let anyone into the house, but I must welcome my girlfriends!" Am I an ill-behaved dog for that?

15. Story

The Nose

It was a special occasion, a round birthday, and we were invited. The whole extended family was present, and of course, my little Yorkshire Terrier lady was allowed to come along. She was cuddled and petted by all the guests as if she were the guest of honor. However, it seemed that my dog didn't enjoy the large restaurant too much. There were too many people and the noise was terrible, with everyone talking at once, which apparently stressed out my dog. All the guests enjoyed their good lunch, and afterwards, we all took a long walk together, which my Yorkie Aischa enjoyed very much. She was able to sniff out the unfamiliar scents and relax in the different environment.

Later, we went back to the restaurant to have coffee. My dog lay down on her prepared blanket next to me and curled up. A nice relative of mine wanted to get closer to my dog and pet her. What none of us expected, including myself at that moment, was that my little agile dog shot up from her spot and nipped the woman's nose with her small snout, making it bleed a little. The relative screamed in horror and surprise. She had known my dog for a long time and never expected something like that from her. She held her nose for a few minutes and looked at my dog in shock. Many of the guests were gossiping, saying that the dog knew exactly whom to nip in the nose. My dog immediately went back to her blanket as if nothing had happened. But thankfully, it was just a small scratch caused by my dog, and the injured woman still received further ridicule from the other guests. She had to hear: "The dog knew exactly whom to nip in the nose. She particularly likes to bite nosy people!"

My dog had simply thought, "I don't like every nose." Does that make her an ill-mannered dog?

16. Story

The Hideout

It was on a New Year's Eve, another year had passed, and it was the first New Year's Eve for our little dog. Once again, it's a story about our little Yorkshire Terrier lady, Aischa.

We had noticed all day that our dog was very nervous and couldn't find any peace. So we hoped that when the loud fireworks started, she wouldn't get scared. We knew that many animals suffer greatly on this day and for a few weeks afterward, that they get panicked. Every time a bang was heard, the dog lady nervously ran around our apartment and searched for a quieter place. Later, we had arranged to meet friends and went to a good Italian restaurant to eat a New Year's Eve menu together, and afterward, we knew we had to go home immediately. We left Aischa alone at home for a short time, which had never bothered her before. We left the radio on so that the young dog always had noises around her and we also lowered the shutters for safety. We thought we had done the best possible for our lady and left the apartment. When we came home later, our little lady was still on the sofa, not greeting us at all. When I stroked her, the dog shook all over. We couldn't do anything for the poor dog, just calm her down. We poured the champagne for the New Year's Eve and noticed that the crackling of the New Year's Eve fireworks was getting more and more intense, and the poor dog became more and more scared. After midnight and a glass of champagne, some congratulations on the phone, we wanted to check on our dog. But the little dog was suddenly gone. We searched the whole apartment, but she couldn't be found. We thought she had to be found, she couldn't just disappear into thin air. We had to search for the frightened animal for a very long time. Eventually, we looked in our wardrobe, and we finally found her. In the farthest and darkest corner, she had laid down on a blanket, totally crouched up, and looked at me with fearful eyes. Her whole body trembled with fear. I took her out and carried her in my arms, but the little one didn't calm down at all. Shortly after we had laid her on the couch and talked to her calmly, she disappeared back into the wardrobe. She rolled up again and stayed hidden in there all night. What a fright the dog gave us, but what did the little dog go through every one of those nights?

In the following New Year's Eves, we always knew where our dog wanted to hide, we never had to search again, it was always the wardrobe, the same dark corner, we always left a sliding door of the wardrobe slightly open for her.

The dog must have thought, "If you out there make such a noise, I want some peace too! Am I an unruly dog because of that? I feel sorry for the animals during this time, that's why I never have New Year's Eve fireworks in my house!"

17. Story

Children

I know another funny story about my two Dachshund puppies, where the female Trixi doesn't quite fit the role. As I mentioned before, I had trouble training the twins. They always came up with something new to annoy me. I was in our garden with the two of them and they were playing together. We have a nice playground in the middle of our housing complex, and on this beautiful summer day, some children were playing there. They wanted to pet my two young Dachshunds and, of course, play with them. I looked around the garden because it suddenly became unusually quiet, and I had to realize that only one dog was still in the garden. Where was the female suddenly? Where had she hidden? I then looked out onto the playground and had to realize that Trixi was with the children, happily playing with them. I immediately brought her back to the garden, and her brother Rocky was happy about it because he wanted to play with her. But it didn't take long and she had disappeared again, of course, she was back with the children. She had dug herself under the fence. I repeatedly closed the gaps, but the female dog always found a new hole to escape. She was an absolutely child-loving dog, which is why she always looked for a way to be with the children. She felt comfortable here! She didn't understand that I wanted to protect her, as there was a road between the garden and the playground and she could have been run over. But that didn't stop Trixi, and her brother Rocky sat sadly in the garden, watching his sister from a safe distance from the garden. His eyes were always fixed on the playground. Playing with children wasn't his thing, he preferred his peace, but wrestling and romping around with his sister, that was something for him!

She just thought, "I like children, what's wrong with that? That doesn't make me a naughty dog!"

18. Story

Breakfast

A funny story that I wouldn't have expected from this dog. A neighbor owned a female Springer Spaniel, with a cozy and well-behaved nature. The older lady always obeyed her every word.

However, whenever we encountered the dog on our walks, we noticed that her nose searched every bag for any hidden snacks. Nothing could be hidden from this dog, as she never missed a good treat. When her keen sense of smell detected something, she begged until she got a small bite. This older lady would not let us leave without a treat. She knew exactly which jacket pocket we kept the good stuff in and who she could beg from, as her hunger was often greater than her good manners!

Now we come to the actual story. As the single woman told us about her dog, she wanted to prepare a small breakfast in her living room after the first walk. She had a low living room table on which she placed jam, butter, and bread. She put a new butter in the container and then went to get a freshly brewed coffee from the kitchen. She didn't waste a thought that her dog could steal something from the table, as the older lady had not done so for a long time, so she was absolutely sure. When she returned with her coffee cup, she couldn't believe her eyes. She saw the dog sitting next to the table, smacking her lips and the butter dish was empty. Had her dog simply pushed the lid of the butter dish aside and snatched half a pound of butter and swallowed it quickly? She couldn't believe that her older lady had eaten such a large piece of butter all at once. Now she had to eat her jam sandwich without butter. The dog sat next to the table with innocent eyes.

 The dog thought that when you're hungry, you have to eat something, and the butter was right in front of my nose on the table. So much butter wouldn't fit on a piece of bread, and there was plenty of room in my stomach.

That's why I wasn't being naughty!

19. Story

The Shopping Trip

 I have another story to offer, which a colleague told me during lunch break and at first, I didn't believe it. A colleague who owned a young Doberman told me about his incredible experience. He wanted to take his young dog for a walk in a different environment, so he took his car and drove to the countryside with him that day. The young dog enjoyed meeting other dogs and could really let off steam. Afterwards, he wanted to drive directly home, but as often happens, he remembered that he had passed a store that might have a specific part he urgently needed. He parked his car in front of the store and went inside. But it took a little longer than he thought, they had to look it up in the computer first and then get the specific part from the warehouse, which was very time-consuming. My colleague became a little restless in the store because he didn't know what his young dog was doing in the car during this time. When he returned to his car, he couldn't believe his eyes. The dog had completely chewed up his car's seat cushions, and foam and fabric shreds were scattered everywhere in the vehicle. The entire interior of the car was thus destroyed. My colleague was stunned as he looked at his car, he had never seen such destructive behavior. It wasn't the first Doberman he had raised, but none of them had ever done anything like this. The dog thought to himself, "If my owner leaves me alone for so long, I have to occupy myself with something, and the seat cushions were absolutely not to my taste, the color of the seats was terrible!"

I'm not an ill-behaved dog, just a little neglected!

20. Story
The Bike Tour

It was a beautiful summer day and we thought to ourselves: "Let's take out our bikes, bring our Aischa along, and head to a lake. Our dog can play with a ball and go in the water."

We quickly packed everything up and got our bikes ready. Our Yorkshire Terrier went into a dog basket that was attached to the handlebars, so I had the little lady always in sight and could quickly intervene if something happened. We set off quickly, and the dog sat quietly in her basket, calmly observing her surroundings. Sometimes she growled when she spotted another dog, but then peace returned to the dog basket. We took a few breaks so the dog could stretch her little paws. Then we continued on to the well-known lake. We passed some meadows where other dogs often frolicked, but my dog wasn't particularly interested. But shortly thereafter, we came to a meadow where some big Dobermans were playing. Suddenly, my little Yorkshire Terrier was totally excited and started barking hysterically, refusing to calm down. The big heads of the huge dogs all turned in my direction, and their massive bodies immediately ran towards me. My dog continued to bark even louder and wouldn't stop. I panicked and thought to myself, "If these huge dogs jump on me because of my dog and start biting, I can only say a prayer, then it's all over for us." I still don't understand exactly what had gotten into my dog at that moment. Furthermore, I had to stop my bike because of my dog's behavior. Suddenly, the giant dogs stopped running and surrounded my bike, all looking into the dog basket. My dog was nowhere to be seen or heard. The hysterical little lady was suddenly lying at the bottom of her basket and remained calm. The owners of the big dogs came calmly over to me and chuckled. They said their dogs didn't do anything. I laughed and replied, "But they have a very calming effect on my dog." I lifted our talkative dog out of the basket in front of the big dogs, nothing happened except that the little one started playing with these huge dogs. My little Yorkshire Terrier could take shelter from rainy weather with her big playmates. After that, we continued on to the lake regardless.

My dog must have thought, "I can choose my own friends even if they're bigger." That's why I'm not an ill-behaved dog after all!

21. Story
Canal Walk

Back then, we had trained our Aischa to walk without a leash and come immediately to us when called, staying by our side. We were very proud that we had taught our Yorkshire Terrier lady this. Since it had worked well along the Wertach river, we thought it would work just as well elsewhere with our Yorkie.

So we put her in our car and drove not too far to the Wertach Canal, where there was a beautiful footpath and some people were out walking their dogs on the weekend. After a few meters, we decided to remove the leash from our little dog. It worked wonderfully, our dog walked obediently beside us.

It didn't take long before the first dogs arrived, they were greeted nicely and they sniffed each other. Then we continued to walk together obediently, everything was so beautiful! We were so proud of our dog, that she was really so well-behaved and walked so nicely with us without a leash. Suddenly, I spotted a gray, large Doberman trotting towards us. The huge magnificent animal walked towards us nonchalantly. The big dog didn't pay any attention to our little one. Suddenly, our little Yorkshire Terrier ran quite boldly under the huge dog, started screaming wildly, and nipped at the big dog's legs. Our hearts fell into our pockets as we watched our little dog nip at the legs of the huge dog, which was almost the size of a small calf. A bite from the huge head of the Doberman and our dog would have been done for. Our cheeky little dog ran at a speed through the legs of the dog, that the Doberman didn't know where it went, until the big bulky body had turned around, our dog was already somewhere else. Our little Yorkshire Terrier kept going after the big dog's legs. We called and screamed, but it didn't help at that moment. We didn't dare to get close to the Doberman, and his owner was helpless. But then the moment came, the Doberman had its huge head over our little dog and barked at her. Suddenly, my little dog was between my legs and trembling. The little devil had probably taken on too much.

We briefly talked to the owners of the Doberman, who was also a female and thankfully gentle. They said, "That our dog was pretty brave, their dog had now set our young dog straight, and hopefully that was a lesson." After that, our dog had to walk on a leash, punishment had to be meted out, and I said to her: "We probably need to practice a bit more."

My dog probably thought, "He can't just walk past without noticing me, I'll show him, he won't do it again!" That's why I'm not an unruly dog!

22. Story
At Home

Afterwards, I remembered a nice story about my first dog, a Yorkshire Terrier. Being totally inexperienced with dog training, we didn't know the peculiarities that a dog could possess, but we tried our luck anyway. Nevertheless, we visited a dog school once a week on Sundays. As I had already described, we tried to teach our dog some things along the Wertach river.

This time, I went alone with our dog to the Wertach river and unleashed Aischa. Everything we trained together went perfectly. But suddenly, my little dog apparently didn't want to anymore. She simply disappeared into the bushes and couldn't be found anymore. Calling and shouting didn't help, the dog had simply vanished. I thought to myself: "She can't just have vanished into thin air, she didn't run away, did she?" Big doubts overcame me as to what I should do next. I continued to ponder: "If I continue to walk, Aischa might be looking for me and run even further away. If she got lost, I have to look for her. What should I do first?" I called the little one, but nothing stirred, no barking, nothing could be heard.

After a long time, I decided: "I'll run home quickly and get my wife's help. Together, we have a better chance of finding her."

I ran back quickly and what did I see there? My dog lay calmly in front of the door and looked at me bored, so to speak: "Where have you been? I've been waiting for you for a long time." Apparently, my dog had just walked comfortably home and thought: "You can do the exercises alone." As soon as I was with our dog in the apartment, she thought: "Playing and romping around would be much nicer now, right?" But I didn't feel like playing at all this time. Playing was no longer on the program. My wife found the incident quite amusing, she said: "At least she didn't just run away, she just went home." But why hadn't I seen her when she ran away?

My dog probably thought: "I didn't feel like learning today, so I'd rather just go home. Tomorrow is another day!" That's how I'm not an ill-behaved dog!

23. Story

Peanuts

After my dachshunds, we had two poodle mixes that my second wife brought with her. They were two older ladies and were twins. One was smaller and more mischievous, and the other was larger, but more relaxed and calm.

The little mischievous one had a habit that I would like to share. Whenever we opened a can of peanuts, Nelli would prick up her ears and immediately come to us. We could do anything with little Nelli. The dog lady was crazy about nuts, no matter what kind of nuts. She would do anything to get a hold of them, just like a squirrel. When I held the nuts over her head, her eyes and her whole head followed them back and forth. Her eyes greedily followed the nut.

I didn't just give her the nuts, I always made her do something for them. We always made a fun game out of it, and we had our fun, and she had the nuts, but we made sure she didn't get too much of them. Training Nelli to do something, like giving a paw, was very easy with a nut.

The little one must have thought: "If you can snack on something like that, then I can do it twice!" That's why I'm not a naughty dog, but a little snacker!

24. Story
Cows

We went on a mountain hike with our Dachshund mixes. The dogs were still very young at the time and had no problems running up the steep mountain, they even had a lot of fun doing it. It was a new experience for them and they were able to burn off their excess energy. There were no incidents until we reached a hut at the top, they walked quite obediently.

When we reached the top, we stopped at a large hut to have something to drink and eat. There was a large meadow all around, and some cows were grazing nearby behind a fence. There was absolutely no danger to our dogs that they could fall or cause any trouble. Other people also let their dogs run freely on the huge meadow. So we thought, let our two dogs play a bit with the other dogs.

But our two dogs had no intention of playing with the other dogs. They were almost constantly roughhousing with each other and playing on the meadow. The other guests found the two young dogs amusing. They never gave up and lay down only for a moment. The cows watched the two young dogs quite bored.

We were just eating when one of the guests called out to us that our dogs were with the cows. These little devils had simply slipped under the fence and barked at the cows together. Most of the cows didn't care about the commotion the two dogs were making. They probably thought, "What do those two stupid dogs want from us!"

But one of the cows had a small calf. She was not to be messed with. When our dogs approached her, the cow yelled at them and ran towards them, stomping her front feet on the ground! We interrupted our meal and immediately ran to the fenced pasture of the cows. We had never seen our dogs run away so quickly.

Squeaking and barking in fear, they ran towards us and just wanted to quickly slip through the fence. Their bravery was gone, they only knew how to flee now. However, the two dogs touched the fence during their escape, and it was electrified. Suddenly, they yelped and cried. It didn't hurt them, but the shock was much worse than the electric shock. They behaved very well and tremblingly let themselves be picked up. We were able to finish our meal and the two dogs didn't make a sound until we decided to start the descent. They quickly forgot the experience and started roughhousing and playing together again. But later we noticed that they were careful around fences and made sure not to get too close.

The dogs thought, we didn't know that these cows had such stupid fences.

That's why we're not misbehaving dogs!

25. Story
The Dog with the Flyswatter

A very peculiar story was told to me by a good friend and neighbor. It's a story that's almost too unbelievable to be true, but she assured me that it happened exactly as she described it.

She had a larger mixed breed dog that she rescued from a laboratory. The dog knew nothing, not even grass or a gentle hand, he was completely traumatized. With a lot of love and patience, she managed to earn his trust and properly train him. However, there was one habit of the dog's that she didn't like: he would wake her up very early in the morning to go for a walk. She talked to her friend about it, who had also rescued a dog from the same laboratory, and this woman suggested, "Go out with him a little later, and if he comes back so early again, just ignore him for a while. Maybe he'll go back to sleep for a few more minutes." Her friend was convinced that this plan would work and that the dog would get used to sleeping a little longer.

So, she confidently went out with her dog very late at night for a walk, and the woman and her dog went to bed afterwards. But as always, her dog stood by her bed and wanted to wake her up. This time, however, the woman refused to give in. She didn't open her eyes or make any attempt to get up. The dog became increasingly restless and refused to give up. He wouldn't lie back down, he whined and ran around. But the woman refused to give in, thinking, "Hopefully he'll give up and go back to sleep for a few more minutes." But what she didn't realize was that "a dog apparently thinks differently."

The dog must have noticed that there was a flyswatter next to the woman's bed. He picked it up in his mouth and swung it over her head, moving only his head. The dog hit her with the flyswatter. The friend recounts that, at that point, there was no choice but to get up and take him for a walk, even though it was difficult. If he didn't see any success, he would just throw the thing at my head until I woke up. She claimed, "I have a dog with a flyswatter, even though it was just a flyswatter!"

The dog thought to himself, "If I want to go outside and I can't wake my owner up, then I have to do something about it. That doesn't make me an unruly dog!"

Epilogue:

It will always be the case, as long as we own and live with animals. No matter what kind of animal we have, there will always be funny stories that come out of it. If we don't have animals, we don't have stories to tell. When a family member, such as a dog or cat, passes away, we immediately feel that something is missing in our environment, in our home or apartment. The owner no longer meets with other dog owners, with whom they often stand around and chat while their dogs play together. So, what does the lonely person do? They usually bring home a new family member, whom they have lots to tell about, and they can introduce their new companion to all the other dog owners. Conversation is once again guaranteed, and they have a loyal companion who will always be there for them. I wish all dog owners many more happy years with their family members, that they will continue to have great fun with their loved ones and that many new funny stories will arise!

Yours faithfully, Peter S. Fischer, loyal dog owner.